KT-571-828

PEMBROKE BRANCH TEL. 6689575

The Hug

A FABER PICTURE BOOK

For Sonny and Cody
P.D.

FABER & FABER has published children's books since 1929. Some of our very first publications included *Old Possum's Book of Practical Cats* by T. S. Eliot starring the now world-famous Macavity, and *The Iron Man* by Ted Hughes. Our catalogue at the time said that 'it is by reading such books that children learn the difference between the shoddy and the genuine'. We still believe in the power of reading to transform children's lives.

First published in the UK in 2019
First published in the US in 2019
by Faber and Faber Limited
Bloomsbury House, 74–77 Great Russell Street, London WC1B 3DA
Text © Eoin McLaughlin, 2019 Illustrations © Polly Dunbar, 2019
Designed by Faber and Faber
US HB ISBN 978–0–571–34875–6
PB ISBN 978–0–571–34001–9
All rights reserved.
Printed in India
10 9 8 7 6 5 4 3 2 1
The moral rights of Eoin McLaughlin and Polly Dunbar have been asserted.
A CIP record for this book is available from the British Library.

Eoin McLaughlin ★ Polly Dunbar

The Hug

PEMBROKE BRANCH TEL. 6689575

Tortoise was feeling sad.
As sad as a tortoise can feel.
So sad only one thing could help.

"Hello," said Tortoise.

"Hello," said Badger.

"Might you give me a big hug?" asked Tortoise.

"I'm sorry, but my hands are sticky," replied Badger.

slurp
guzzle
slurp.

"Might I trouble *you* for a small hug?"
asked Tortoise.

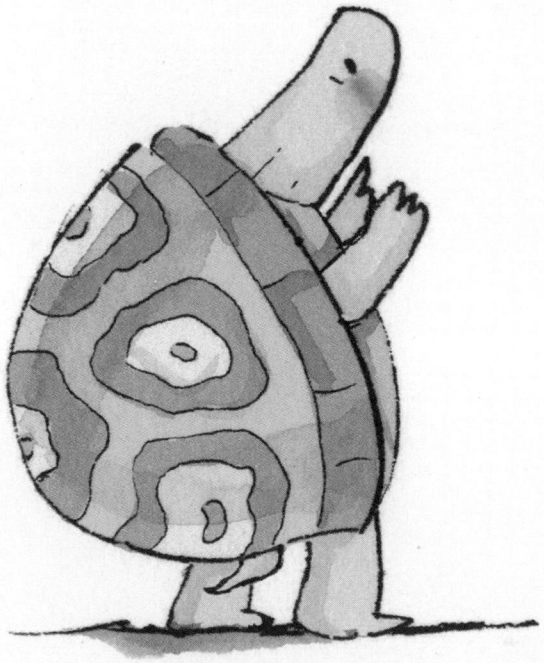

"Not right now,"
said Rabbit.
"Unfortunately
I'm digging a very
important hole."

Dig
Dig

PEMBROKE BRANCH TEL. 6689575

"Do *you* have time for a quick hug?"
asked Tortoise.

"Not today," replied Frog. "Sorry,
but I have to jump over there now."

Boing!

"Why will no one hug me?" asked Tortoise.

"It's your shell," replied Owl.
"It's just so very hard.
But don't worry.
There's someone
for everyone."

"Now I am even more sad," said Tortoise.
"Will I *ever* find someone to hug?"

And that's when . . .

they

met.

And . . . that's . . .

when . . . they . . .

PEMBROKE BRANCH TEL. 6689575

. . . hugged . . .

As happy as a hug
can make you . . .

As happy as two
someones can be.

when . . . they . . .

And . . . that's . . .

met.

they

And that's when . . .

"Now I am even more sad," said Hedgehog.
"Will I *ever* find someone to hug?"

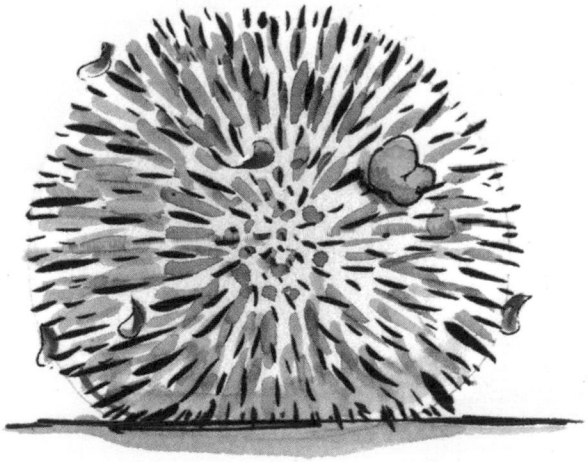

"You're just a little bit tricky to hug," replied Owl, "with all your prickly prickles. But don't worry, there's someone for everyone."

"Why will no one hug me?" Hedgehog sniffed.

wkkkk Sqquawk Squawk

Sssqquuaawwwkkk ssssquua

"Perhaps after I sing my song,"
replied Magpie, "which is quite long."

"Might *you* give me just a small hug?"
begged Hedgehog.

PEMBROKE BRANCH TEL. 6689575

"Now I'll have to start over.
One . . . Two . . . Three . . ."

"I'm a little busy
counting all of
my nuts,"
replied Squirrel,

who only had
three nuts.

"I'm feeling quite sad and would *very* much like a hug," said Hedgehog.

CRASH!
SPLAT!

BANG!

"I'd love to," replied Fox,
"but I've just got to
knock over that bin."

"Please may I have a hug?" asked Hedgehog.

"Hello," said Fox.

"Hello," said Hedgehog.

Hedgehog was feeling sad.
As sad as a hedgehog can feel.
So sad only one thing could help.

Eoin McLaughlin ♥ Polly Dunbar

The Hug

PEMBROKE BRANCH TEL. 668957

Leabharlanna Poiblí Chathair Baile Atha Cliath
Dublin City Public Libraries

A FABER PICTURE BOOK

For Rach
E.M.

FABER & FABER has published children's books since 1929. Some of our very first publications included *Old Possum's Book of Practical Cats* by T. S. Eliot starring the now world-famous Macavity, and *The Iron Man* by Ted Hughes. Our catalogue at the time said that 'it is by reading such books that children learn the difference between the shoddy and the genuine'. We still believe in the power of reading to transform children's lives.

First published in the UK in 2019
First published in the US in 2019
by Faber and Faber Limited
Bloomsbury House, 74–77 Great Russell Street, London WC1B 3DA
Text © Eoin McLaughlin, 2019 Illustrations © Polly Dunbar, 2019
Designed by Faber and Faber
US HB ISBN 978-0-571-34875-6
PB ISBN 978-0-571-34001-9
All rights reserved.
Printed in India
10 9 8 7 6 5 4 3 2 1
The moral rights of Eoin McLaughlin and Polly Dunbar have been asserted.
A CIP record for this book is available from the British Library.

90 YEARS OF EXCELLENCE
FABER & FABER

The Hug

Withdrawn from Stock
Dublin City Public Libraries